Using

When going
with your child, you can either read through
the story first, talking about it
and discussing the pictures,
or start with the sounds pages
at the beginning.

If you start at the front of the book,
read the words and point to the pictures.
Emphasise the **sound** of the letter.

Encourage your child to think
of the other words beginning with
and including the same sound.
The story gives you the opportunity
to point out these sounds.

After the story, slowly go through the
sounds pages at the end.

Always praise and encourage
as you go along. Keep your
reading sessions short and stop
if your child loses interest.

Throughout the series, the order in which the sounds
are introduced has been carefully planned to
help the important link between reading and writing.
This link has proved to be a powerful boost to
the development of both skills.

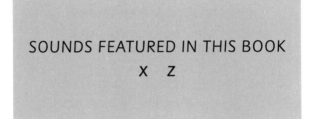

SOUNDS FEATURED IN THIS BOOK

x   z

The sounds introduced are repeated
and given emphasis in the practice books,
where the link between reading and writing is at the
root of the activities and games.

Ladybird books are widely available, but in case of
difficulty may be ordered by post or telephone from:

Ladybird Books – Cash Sales Department
Littlegate Road Paignton Devon TQ3 3BE
Telephone 0803 554761

A catalogue record for this book is available
from the British Library

Published by Ladybird Books Ltd Loughborough Leicestershire UK
Ladybird Books Inc Auburn Maine 04210 USA

Printed in EC

Say the Sounds
The accident

by JILL CORBY

illustrated by PETER WILKS

Xx

x-ray

box

fox

Wex

Say the sound.

six

mix

fix

wax

ox

Zz

buzz

doze

zoo

zebra

6

zip

freeze

quiz

dizzy

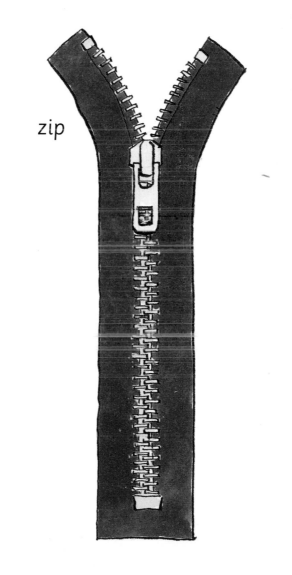

"Mum, as it's a lovely morning, can we go to the zoo?" asked Jenny.

"Yes, I want to go to the zoo, too," Ben told his mum.

"We want to see all the creatures in the zoo," they told her.

"Please can we go this morning?"
Ben asked.

"Yes, we want to go this morning,
please," Jenny said.

"Right. We will all have a lovely
day at the zoo," Dad told them.

So they went to the zoo that lovely day.

When they were in the car, Mum looked at the map.

"We have to go right just here," she told Dad.

So Dad turned right before the hill.

"Where is the zoo now?" he asked.

"It's up this hill on the right,"
Mum said, looking at the map.

Then, before the blue car, Dad
turned right into the car park.

"What a lot of rights," said Ben
to himself.

"It's a very big car park with lots of cars," Ben said. Then they all walked from the car park to the zoo.

But just before they got there, something happened. It happened very quickly.

There were lots of stones everywhere but there was one little stone and Jenny didn't see it. No one saw it but Jenny happened to step on it and fell over. She put out her arm as she fell and hurt it badly.

"It's not going to be a lovely day at all," said Ben to himself.

Dad picked Jenny up and walked back to the car. Her arm hurt badly, but she was very brave, and tried to keep still. Ben picked up the little stone and looked at it. It was only little. He picked up the one that he had just walked on.

It was little, too. How could Jenny have hurt her arm so badly?

"Right. Now off we go to the hospital," Dad told them.

"And we won't get to the zoo at all," said Ben to himself.

At the hospital the nurse said,
"I shall take an X-ray of your arm
like this. And then I shall take one
like that," and she turned Jenny's
arm over.

"Then we shall see if you have
any broken bones. You won't
move, will you? Keep very still."

She was very nice to Jenny and didn't hurt her at all.

"I shall take lots of X-rays so that the doctor can see if any bones are broken," the nurse said. "You are a brave girl."

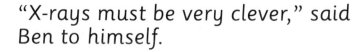

"X-rays must be very clever," said Ben to himself.

The nurse gave the doctor the X-rays. He looked at them. Ben looked at them, too.

"The doctor must be very clever," he said.

"Shall we see if any bones are broken?" the doctor asked.
"Yes, Jenny. You have broken one bone in your arm," he told her.

"We will have to put a plaster cast on it so that the bones won't move."

Jenny didn't look very pleased.

"Won't it hurt if you put a plaster cast on it?" she asked.

"Not at all," the doctor told her. "Keep still and don't move your arm, now."

Then they put a plaster cast on her arm.

"Be brave, Jenny," said Ben to himself.

When Jenny went home from the hospital it was time for bed. She was very tired and fell asleep quickly.

Then a strange thing happened. She was not tired any more. Not tired at all. And she was not asleep. Not asleep at all.

It was time
to go to the
zoo with Ben.
They walked in and
saw the monkeys first.
The clever monkeys were
swinging high up in the trees. Ben
and Jenny climbed the trees to go
swinging with them.

Jenny's arm didn't hurt at all. She
looked very well. Swinging
monkeys chased them and then
Ben and Jenny chased the monkeys.
They chased high up in the trees.
They laughed and laughed and had
a lovely time.

They saw a big green and red snake.
He was high in the trees as well.

Then they saw the elephant.

"I want to go riding on it," Ben told her. So Jenny put her plaster arm out to help him to climb up.

The elephant put Jenny on his back as well and they went riding down the hill.

They saw the octopus in the water. She didn't look very pleased. Then Ben saw why.

"Look, Jenny. She has been caught by that yellow shell. She can't move away from the shell.

"One of her tentacles has been caught and she can't move at all," Ben went on.

Ben tried to open the yellow shell. But he could not do it. Then Jenny had an idea.

"I shall make that shell open and get your tentacle out," Jenny told the octopus. "If I put my plaster arm in the shell, it should open and the tentacle should come out."

Jenny tried to get her arm into the shell. She tried hard to get it in. Then she roared at the yellow shell. It was so surprised and scared that it opened quickly and the tentacle came out.

The octopus was very pleased that the shell had opened.

They saw the dolphins in the
water. Ben and Jenny caught one
and round and round the pool
they went. Then Jenny put her
plaster arm out so that the
dolphins could jump right over it.
She laughed at the dolphins going
round in the water.

Next they came to the ostrich.

"What a big bird that is," Ben said.

"Look over there, Ben. That bird has made a nest," Jenny told him.

They could see that the bird had some eggs. Three huge ostrich eggs were in the nest.

Then they saw a big crocodile
going quietly up to the nest with
the three huge ostrich eggs.

"What is he going to do?" Ben
asked Jenny quietly.

"He looks as if he wants to eat
one of the eggs," she told him.

Ben and Jenny looked as the crocodile went very quietly up to the three eggs. He opened his jaws and they could see all his sharp teeth. He was going to eat an egg.

Then Jenny knew what she had to do. She had to stop the crocodile. He was going to eat the ostrich eggs.

The crocodile opened his huge jaws once more.

She ran at him and shouted, "Go away. Go away. Right away."
And she swung her plaster arm.

She swung it round hard at the crocodile's jaw. She swung at his jaw so hard that it hurt him. The crocodile didn't like it and walked away quickly.

The next thing that Jenny knew
was that her dad was by her with
some tea.

"How are you this morning?" he
asked. "Does your arm hurt?"

"I have been to the zoo," she told him. "I had a lovely time."

"Well, I don't know how you did it!" Dad told her. "You have been fast asleep all the time!"

Zz

Say what these things are. When can you hear the Z sound?

Z

Read these words.

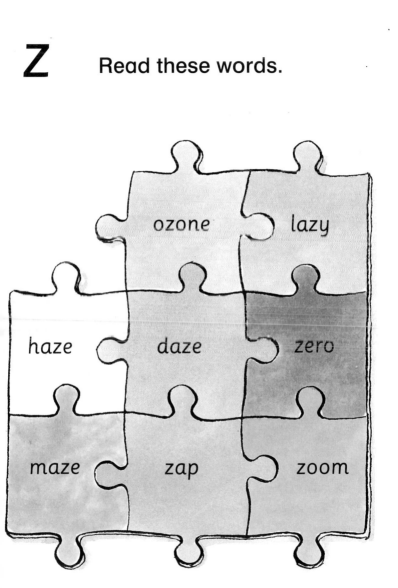

ozone   lazy

haze   daze   zero

maze   zap   zoom

X

Read these.
The pictures will help.

The ox and the fox explore
in their socks.

Wex picks up six sticks.

X

Can you read these words?
Do you know what
they mean?

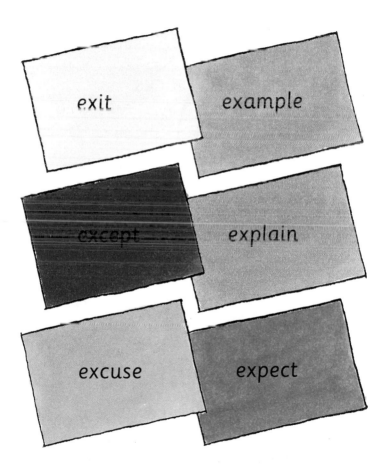

exit

example

except

explain

excuse

expect

cks Makes a sound like X.

sacks

ticks

licks

socks

tricks

bricks

blocks

backs

tacks

chicks

flicks

kicks

sticks

New words used in the story

Words introduced 60

Learn to read with Ladybird

Read with me

A scheme of 16 graded books which uses a look-say approach to introduce beginner readers to the first 300 most frequently used words in the English language (Key Words). Children learn whole words and, with practice and repetition, build up a reading vocabulary.

Support material: Pre-reader, Practice and Play Books, Book and Cassette Packs, Picture Dictionary, Picture Word Cards

Say the Sounds

A phonically based, graded reading scheme of 8 titles. It teaches children the sounds of individual letters and letter combinations, enabling them to feel confident in approaching Key Words.

Support material:
Practice Books, Double Cassette Pack, Flash Cards

Read it yourself

A graded series of 24 books to help children to learn new words in the context of a familiar story. These readers follow on from the pre-reading series, **Read together**, and can be used in conjunction with any Ladybird reading scheme.